TOMMY COCKLE
AND *THE PORTAL TO LAVA AND ICE*

BY **EDDIE COLLMAN**
INSPIRED BY **ADAM** & **SAM COLLMAN**

TYPESET IN KOMIKA AND DANTE

ILLUSTRATIONS BY CHRIS ACUÑA

EDITING, DESIGN, TYPESETTING AND PUBLISHING BY UK BOOK PUBLISHING

ISBN: 978-1-912183-24-1

WWW.UKBOOKPUBLISHING.COM

TOMMY COCKLE

AND THE PORTAL TO LAVA AND ICE

ACKNOWLEDGEMENTS

The adventures in this book came from the minds of my wonderful twin boys, *Adam* and *Sam*. Love you so much

Lots of love and thanks to *Sahra Kirk* and *Joan Collman* for proofreading and support

"MY NAME IS SID. MY BEST FRIEND IS CALLED TOMMY COCKLE. WE ARE INSEPARABLE"

CHAPTER 1:
MY BEST FRIEND

Tommy Cockle (Tom as he's known) never had any brothers or sisters. But, he has me.

My name is Sid. I am Tom's best friend. We are inseparable.

Tom and I were born on the same day. Of course I don't remember Tom back then but we've always been together.

Tom is a nice guy. He always says and does the right things.

Let me give you an example: When a teacher shouts at Tom for something he hasn't done, Tom immediately says "sorry" and carries on with his work. If Tom stubs his toe he pulls a funny screwed up face but he doesn't cry out. When a bully calls Tom names he just looks down and walks away.

I, however, am different. If a teacher shouts at me and

it isn't my fault I shout back. If I stub my toe I holler and scream. If someone calls me names I call them names back. Of course no one hears.

Tom and I were born ten years ago on the fifth of July. We have always shared birthday parties and always will. We love having birthdays as it makes us feel special. We love feeling special. When we feel special with that wonderful bubbly sparkly feeling in our tummies we are as one.

But most of the time we are very different.

The first time I remember Tom and I being together was sitting on a swing at a playground near our house in Hillingbourne. It was a sad day. Auntie Jayne and Uncle Jack had just broken the sad news that Mum and Dad had gone to heaven, but they would always be looking down on us and would always love us very much. As Tom sat on the swing looking at the ground he felt sad and upset. That is my first memory of us being together. Just him and me, swinging backwards and forwards in that playground.

I think of myself as the Tom that Tom wants to be sometimes. Only Tom hears and sees me. He is my best friend.

By the way, we call Mum 'Moon' and Dad 'Star'. Tom finds it easier to call them this because if he says Mum and Dad it sometimes makes us cry.

Tom and I do cry sometimes. We cry at strange times of the day. Sometimes we cry in the middle of class. But nowadays Tom lets me cry alone so that the class won't see him sobbing.

Another reason Tom calls them Moon and Star is when we look up into the sky at night we can see them looking down on us. It makes us feel sad and happy at the same time, which is quite a confusing feeling to have.

But that's enough about that. I love Tom very much. He is my best buddy.

CHAPTER 2:
THE DARK SIDE OF THE FOREST

T om and I are very different but that has never stopped us having the most amazing adventures together. Our adventures are the most amazing supersonic cranbabulous adventures that boys could ever have. By the way I made up the word cranbabulous, but I reckon you already knew that.

Tom and I live in a big house on a busy main road just outside the centre of town. We live with Uncle Jack and Auntie Jayne. Our house is positioned on the corner of Blabalab Forest. Which is a name clearly made up by a crazy person! But it's great because it means we can play in the forest together when we come home from school. We don't like school. The main reason for this is the teachers… and other pupils!

Well, maybe not all the teachers and pupils, but some.

Mrs Butterfly is a nice teacher. She can shout and scream at the class sometimes, but we know she cares deep down. Kids somehow just know when a teacher is nice. Tom and I both like her very much.

Mrs Craddlethorpe is not a nice teacher. She once kept us back from school for a whole hour for something we didn't do! I was furious and I told her exactly what I thought, although of course Mrs Craddlethorpe didn't hear me. Tom just said nothing.

It was on Friday the fourth of July, the day before our tenth birthday, when Uncle Jack said we could play in the forest on our own. "Now be sure not to stray too far from the house," Uncle Jack said before we were allowed out. Uncle Jack is nice. He is a big portly man with small feet. Tom and I worry sometimes that he might topple over. If he did topple over I think he would find it hard to get up.

Auntie Jayne is nice too. She is Moon's sister. Auntie Jayne tends to worry a lot about everything, but we know she cares. She says most days, "Tom. Are you OK, is there anything you want to talk about?" Tom normally says no, whereas I have many things that I want to know and discuss. As you probably now realise, she hears nothing.

It was about 6pm by the time we went out to play. Uncle Jack had told us to be home by 8 o'clock at the latest when it would start to get dark. "Stay out of the dark forest!" Uncle Jack shouted as we ran out of the house.

The forest was divided into two sections. The first section we called *the light forest*, which was just like a normal park with a playground and some great climbing trees. The second and much more exciting section we called *the dark forest*. It was exactly as you would imagine it to be. It was dark, very dark. The trees were so tall and bushy that the sunshine could only light up little bits at a time. I loved the darker sections. Tom thought they were very scary.

There was a stream that ran through the middle of the dark forest, which we were strictly forbidden to ever cross. Uncle Jack said that some people who crossed the stream had got lost in the forest on the other side and never returned. We don't believe this. We think Uncle Jack says this because he is scared too.

I also think that Uncle Jack is mad to tell us not to cross the stream. When someone tells me not to do something I see it as something I have to do! Tom, however, never breaks the rules so we've never been to the other side of the stream.

When we went outside a few children were kicking a football around in the light forest. "Hey Tom, fancy a kick around?" one of the boys shouted across. I was keen to play but Tom replied softly, "No thanks." Tom always

7

says no. I love Tom but I wish we could play with other kids sometimes.

Just then, one of the boys kicked the ball into the dark forest by a large overgrown tree right next to where we were standing. Tom walked across to retrieve the ball, and as he bent down to pick it up we heard a scuffle from underneath the tree. "What is it?" I whispered. "I'm not sure," replied Tom.

"Tom, get the ball," one of the boys shouted over, eager to carry on with his game. Tom retrieved the ball and threw it back to the boys.

We stood next to the dark forest. "Let's go in and take a look," I whispered to Tom. Tom was cautious; he didn't like disobeying anyone, particularly Uncle Jack. "But we are not supposed to," he whispered back.

"What if it's an animal that needs our help?" I said to Tom. Now, I should tell you that Tom loves animals, so suggesting it might be an animal was always going to pull at his heart strings.

Tom sighed. "OK," he said reluctantly. "But we mustn't lose sight of the light forest."

We kneeled down by the large tree and slowly crawled our way in under the huge branches.

The forest seemed darker than usual. "I don't think this is a good idea!" Tom said. He sounded afraid. "Nonsense," I replied.

We continued crawling on our hands and knees, following the rustling noise that was leading us deeper into the dark forest. Many of the overgrown trees and bushes were prickly; their thorns seemed to be scratching at us every time we moved.

"My knees are filthy with mud!" Tom said. "Keep going," I whispered, "I can see the bushes moving just in front of us!"

Deeper we went. As the trees and bushes around us became thicker the light was beginning to fade.

Tom paused. He looked around. "Sid," he said, "I can't see any daylight behind us!"

Tom was right. We must have been crawling for

a while. The scuffling noise was following a familiar pattern. Every time we stopped the noise seemed to stop too. Every time we started crawling we would hear the noise moving further away.

"Let's keep going, Tom. We've come this far and we can't turn back now," I said. "I think we are close to whatever is making that sound!"

CHAPTER 3:

THE STREAM

As we continued to crawl, the lower branches of the trees were becoming a little easier to navigate. "I think we've entered a clearing, Tom," I whispered.

We stood up and looked around. It was quiet. The scuffling noise had stopped. All we could hear was the sound of birds singing; we could no longer hear the busy main road by our house. "Great, I think we are lost!" Tom said, sarcastically. "Rubbish," I replied, "come on, let's keep going."

"Which way do you think we should go?" Tom said. He looked a little tired and fed up.

I had no idea. "I think we should go this way," I said as I closed my eyes and hoped for the best. Tom often asked me what we should do. He often avoids my advice, but this time for some reason he followed me into the clearing.

"Can you hear that, Sid?" Tom whispered. "It sounds like running water."

We had found the stream.

The stream was beautiful. People say that water is clear but this stream was full of colour. Where the thin sun rays reflected on the water it was a beautiful sea blue, and as the light faded the blue turned green then orange. There were many rocks in the stream and the water had to adjust its path to get by. This is what made the noise. It almost felt like the water was complaining as it had to amend its planned route downstream to get past the pesky rocks. Our imagination was fun sometimes.

"Where do you think the animal went?" I asked.

"We don't know that it was an animal," Tom replied, as we stood together looking into the patterns in the stream.

"I think it went over the little rocks," I said pointing to the other side of the stream.

Tom's eyes were transfixed on the water. He was deep in thought. "You want us to go across, don't you?" he said, somewhat warily.

Tom knew what I was saying. I think he viewed me as the naughty one, but deep down he wanted to do it too.

Tom looked up from the water. "What about Uncle Jack? He told us never to cross the stream." Tom hated disobeying the rules. He especially hated disobeying Uncle Jack.

"Let's do it, Tom!" I said, trying my best to sound convincing.

Tom sighed. "OK."

I was shocked! This was the first time that we had ever gone across the stream. We had been to the stream a few times with Uncle Jack and Auntie Jayne, but never over it.

"How shall we get across?" Tom asked. "Let's jump across the little rocks," I replied.

As we approached the water's edge our shoes slid into thick squishy mud.

"Yuck!" Tom said. His face looked as though he was eating a sour sweet.

We tiptoed and jumped our way across the stream; as we looked down, little fish with wavy tails seemed to be looking up at us from the water.

Fish are funny creatures. They wriggle around endlessly. We used to have a fish called Nigel. He used to wriggle over to the side of his tank and talk to us for hours, although he only used to say the word 'Bob', or at least that is what it looked like. One day Nigel died. Fish don't live very long. I think Nigel died of boredom, although Moon told us he died because our cat spilt fish food into the tank and he ate too much. Our cat was called 'Whiskers'. I like that name. Star named her Whiskers because her whiskers were always huge, even when she was young. I like the name Whiskers because you have to make a blowing noise at the start of her name! 'Whhhhiskers!' We also had a dog called 'Larry' and stick insects called 'Norma', 'Boss', 'Malcolm' and 'Glasses'. I miss our pets.

Suddenly Tom shouted "Stop" above the noise of the running water. "Over there!" He was pointing to what looked like an entrance to a cave on the dangerous side of the dark forest.

We paused. Our shoes and socks were now well and truly saturated with water.

"I think we should go in," I said.

Tom looked unsure. "Do you think it is safe?" Tom's voice was a little shaky although he actually seemed quite calm.

"It's too late to turn back," I replied.

We moved closer to the mouth of the cave. "This could be a tunnel to the centre of the world," I said. Tom carried on walking. By this time we had gone under the large rock and Tom gently pulled the branches to one side and peered in.

The cave was damp and cold. It also smelled a little funny. The darkness in the cave was only occasionally broken by the sunshine reflecting in from the stream outside.

"We need a torch," Tom said.

"No need," I replied. "Look over there."

CHAPTER 4:
THE GOLDEN EAGLE

As we walked further into the cave, and looked down into the darkness, we could make out a faint golden light in the distance. In the middle of the golden light, there was a little red glow. "What is that?" Tom whispered. It was magical and mesmerising, something that we hadn't ever seen before. "I don't know," I replied. "But it seems to be getting closer!"

The golden light was indeed getting closer; it was a beautiful, bright, golden sunshine colour. The type of sunshine you see at dusk when the sun is disappearing for the night.

I always imagined the sun was a torch that someone was shining into the sky. Apparently if you look at the sun for too long you can go blind. Our neighbour Doctor Quiz was blind. He had a white stick, which he used to tap on the ground as he walked. I always thought this stick was for his guide dog to play with in the park. Star corrected me on this years ago. I like Doctor Quiz; he always had a story to tell us. His dad was called Tom, which is great. Good for him. He has a fantastic name.

Tom and I stood perfectly still. As the golden light came closer I whispered to Tom, "It looks like some kind of bird?" Tom's eyes were mesmerized by the image coming towards us. "Shush," he said. "I think you're right, it is a bird of some kind, an eagle maybe, it looks like a golden eagle."

It was beautiful.

I had seen gold before. Moon had a golden wedding ring that she was very proud of. It was real gold, but it never shone like this. By now the eagle was in full view. It paused. We were still. Who was going to make the next move? The eagle gently tilted its head to one side then the other, blinking its eyes as it did so. I think it could see us both. Its beak was shiny, very long with a pointy end. There was a red shiny stone in the middle of its plumed chest. The stone seemed to be moving all the time. In fact it was moving really fast, almost beating. "Wow. I think I can see its heart," I whispered to Tom.

The eagle had moved forwards and was now just in front of us. It looked annoyed. I think large birds do look annoyed most of the time. The eagle extended its neck and head towards Tom. We could now see its colours up close. Its body was full of thousands and thousands of little golden feathers, tightly bunched together. The colours twinkled in the sun's rays that were reflecting into the cave from the stream outside. The beating of its ruby red heart was almost hypnotic.

The eagle plumped out its chest and opened its mouth. We held our breath.

"I think it's going to speak," I whispered to Tom.

Tom said nothing.

"SQQQQQQWWWWWAAAAARRRRRK!" it cried.

Tom and I jumped.

"SQQQQQQWWWWWAAAAARRRRRK!" it cried again, this time louder. The echo from its cries gently faded into the depths of the cave.

Tom stood still. He was looking straight at the eagle.

"What shall we do?" I whispered to Tom. "Maybe we should run."

The eagle cried out again.

Suddenly Tom started gently raising his arm towards the eagle. The eagle took an uncertain step backwards. "What are you doing, Tom?" I whispered.

Tom was calm, really calm. He seemed to find an inner strength. He moved his hand higher towards the bird's head, slowly stepping forward as he did so. Then, incredibly slowly and gently, he placed his fingers and then palm onto the side of the eagle's soft, golden face.

I was aghast. He showed such courage.

At Tom's touch, the bird seemed to relax.

Tom began speaking to the bird. "Hello, I'm Tom, do you understand me?"

Silence fell into the cave. No one moved.

"I know who you are," the eagle replied in a deep soft voice, "I've been expecting you."

"It talks!" I screamed. "Ask him something else."

Tom gulped! His hand was still resting on the eagle's face "What is your name?" Tom asked. His body was perfectly still.

"I am Porlo, Guardian of the portals. I have been expecting you, Tom."

"What do you mean *expecting me*?" replied Tom. "How did you know I was coming? We followed a noise, which we believed to be an animal, which led us by chance to here, to this cave!"

Porlo starred at Tom, looked at the ground, and then gently eased his neck forward so his face was right in front of Tom's.

"That was no accident, Tom," said Porlo. "I brought you here."

Tom seemed confused. "So why did you 'squawk' at me when I arrived?" enquired Tom. His head had moved backwards away from Porlo.

"I needed to test you, Tom," said Porlo. "I needed to

test your reaction to potential danger, to see if you were ready."

Porlo bent down and began preening some of his feathers.

"Ready for what?" asked Tom.

"You'll see." With that the eagle turned around and proceeded to walk back down into the dark cave.

"Follow me," he said.

CHAPTER 5:

INTO THE CAVE

Tom and I stood together at the entrance to the cave. "What should we do?" Tom whispered to me. "Follow him," I said.

Tom looked unsure.

"Why should we trust you?" Tom shouted. Porlo paused; he slowly turned his head towards us. "Do what you like," he said. "But if you don't follow me you'll never know."

This felt like a tough decision. Tom and I had faced difficult decisions before. Once, Moon and Star had taken us to a huge ice cream parlour and let us choose three of the most delicious ice cream flavours to put on our super massive ice cream cone. I counted, and there were seventy six delicious flavours to choose from! I chose: Sticky Toffee Sundae, Triple Chocolate Delight and Gooey Fudge Surprise. Tom wanted Vanilla, Strawberry and Chocolate Mint. So that is what we had. I wish Tom was more adventurous sometimes.

"I think we should do it, Tom!" I whispered.

Tom looked unsure. "I know how adventurous you are, Sid, but how can we be sure it's safe? Remember what Moon said about trusting strangers?"

Tom was right. Moon and Star would often talk to us about 'stranger danger', as they called it. We were also shown many programmes at school on how to deal with potentially dangerous situations. I got bored when we watched these programmes but Tom always paid the utmost attention to them.

"Moon also said that you should trust your instinct, Tom," I said. "You can never be certain in life. But you are my best friend, and I love seeing you happy. Take a chance. Let's trust Porlo."

"OK," Tom replied as he walked off into the cave behind Porlo.

I was shocked! It was wonderful to see Tom like this. He normally needed convincing if we were to do anything different but this time he was taking the lead. I was impressed.

We followed a few steps behind Porlo. The cave floor was slippery. "Tread carefully!" Porlo shouted.

As we walked, all around us was deathly silent apart from a noise coming from Porlo.

"Can you hear that?" I whispered to Tom.

"Yes, it's the bird," Tom replied.

"Ask him what he's doing," I said.

"I'm singing," replied Porlo. "And don't call me 'the bird'!"

Tom and I stopped.

"You can hear me?" I asked.

"Of course I can hear you. You're Sid," Porlo replied.

Tom and I looked at each other. "No one has ever heard me before!"

"Well, guess what, I can hear you so get used to it," Porlo replied. "And in answer to your question, I am singing, it happens a lot! I sing when I'm happy, in fact I sing when I'm happy, sad, miserable and angry. Basically I sing most of the time... except when I'm eating!"

Tom smiled.

Tom also likes singing. Or rather Tom used to like singing. He would sing all day if he could. In the bath, in the car, even in the toilet! Everywhere you could think of, Tom would sing. Sometimes Moon would join in and Tom would sing with her for hours. Sadly Tom hasn't sung for a long time. I know why he doesn't sing. He misses her. It makes me sad.

We all continued walking deeper into the cave. "What exactly are these portals and where do they lead?" I shouted to Porlo. By now his singing had become much louder.

Porlo stopped singing. "Good question," he replied.

His singing continued.

"So what are they? These portals?" I asked again.

"Do you think I'd forgotten to answer?" Porlo snapped.

Suddenly a small mouse ran out from a tiny hole at the bottom of the cave, right next to Tom and me. As quick as a flash Porlo threw out his long leg and pinned the mouse to the ground with his claw.

Porlo looked at us. His eyes began to close but stopped halfway, creating an evil glare. He opened his mouth. "You gonna eat that?" he said.

We paused.

"No," Tom replied.

"Good," he said.

With that, Porlo flicked the mouse into the air and straight into his long golden beak; he didn't seem to chew at all and within seconds the mouse was gone. "You should try it sometime," Porlo said as he continued walking into the cave.

Porlo seemed content as he began singing again. "Nearly there," he sang out merrily. "Patience, boys, all will be revealed."

I looked at Tom. His mouth had begun to move in time with Porlo.

"Are you singing?" I asked him.

Tom smiled. He seemed happy.

CHAPTER 6:
THE PORTALS

Porlo was quite a character. For some reason Tom and I really liked him.

"Ask him something else," I whispered to Tom.

"I can hear you, you know!" shouted Porlo.

"Sorry, force of habit. So how old are you?"

"Old enough to know that you should never ask someone my age how old they are," he snapped.

"One hundred years old?" I asked, cheekily!

Porlo stopped. He looked around and gave us one of his evil glares.

"Close enough," he said, "although there might be another zero in there somewhere!"

"How old are you?" Porlo asked.

"Ten," Tom replied. "We are ten."

"You're ten on July fifth." Porlo paused; he looked thoughtful. "Which is tomorrow!"

"Why did you ask us then, if you already knew?" Tom asked.

"Just having fun," said Porlo. He seemed happy that he was right.

"Porlo is pretty strange," I whispered to Tom.

"I can still hear you!" snapped Porlo, merrily singing away to himself.

We had an Uncle Leonard who was also quite strange, crazy in fact, although Moon told us we weren't allowed to call him crazy. "Uncle Leonard is eccentric in a nice way," she would say. Uncle Leonard would often tell stories about the war and the good old days, which Tom found fascinating, but sometimes Moon said he would go over the top with his stories and say things that weren't suitable for children. Apparently Uncle Leonard liked Whisky. This is another word Tom and I like, as you have to make the blowing sound to say it. "Whhhhisky!"

Uncle Leonard eventually had to move into a home, which we found confusing as he already lived in one!

As we continued walking we started to see some bright lights coming from the other end of the cave.

"Where are those lights coming from?" I shouted to Porlo.

"Ah," he said, seemingly pleased with the question. "These are the very reason I brought you here. This is where the adventures begin. Welcome to my portals," Porlo said. He seemed excited.

The cave had suddenly widened. We were in the middle of a huge circle, surrounded by what appeared to be little doorways exploding and shimmering with colour and light. I counted. There were ten doorways.

"Have a look in one. Go on," Porlo said.

"But you've not told us anything about these portals yet, Porlo. Where do they lead to?" Tom said.

"Imagination is key, Tom," he replied.

"What does that even mean?" Tom said, seemingly irritated by Porlo's lack of information.

Porlo smiled. "Trust me, Tom." he said.

"We've come this far," I whispered to Tom.

Tom was clearly in deep thought. He paused. He

looked back at me and then at Porlo and smiled.

"Which one shall we pick?" he said excitedly.

I knew this was going to be fun for Tom. I was pleased.

"Just look around," I shouted, as I ran from door to door looking at the portals.

"There's too many," Tom cried.

"Let's just close our eyes and pick one," I suggested.

We stood with our eyes closed, span around a few times, and randomly pointed to a doorway.

We opened our eyes.

"Ah, a very good choice. A very good choice indeed," Porlo said. "The portal to Lava and Ice."

CHAPTER 7:
THE PORTAL TO LAVA AND ICE

We slowly made our way to the portal across the wet cave floor, and stood in front of the shimmering, glistening entrance. "Take a look," Porlo said. "Go on, be brave!"

Tom and I put our heads through the lights into the portal to Lava and Ice. Light flashed, loud claps of thunder filled our ears.

"What can you see?" Porlo shouted from the cave behind us.

"It's beautiful," replied Tom, shouting back. "I can see a huge volcano, shooting out hundreds and hundreds of hot molten rocks; some are falling onto me but it doesn't hurt for some reason. All the hot magma trails coming from the volcano are shaped like the most amazing slides; the slides seem to go all the way around the mountain. Then each one has a different, most amazing jump at the end. The jumps seem to turn into frozen icy tunnels that go round and around. I can see loads of animals having fun on the slides, whizzing and jumping around. Over there I can see penguins and polar bears speeding along the icy slides. Exotic colourful birds are flying overhead."

"Do you want to go in?" Porlo shouted.

"Yes," Tom replied, "I really do" and with that we began moving forward.

Suddenly Tom and I were tugged back into the cave through the portal, falling onto the cold, wet floor with a bump.

"Not until you've listened to what I have to say," Porlo said. His tone of voice had changed. He began pacing backwards and forwards around the cave. He looked serious.

"When we first met I needed to test your reaction to potential danger. You did well. But the dangers that lurk beyond these portal doors are far greater than anything you have ever experienced before."

Tom and I looked at each other. We had experienced danger before, but not like this. Once when Tom and I were in our old car with Star, a lorry nearly crashed into us on a busy main road. Star shouted out a swear word, which we are never to repeat! He also said that cars were dangerous and that we should "always assume that every driver on the road is an idiot. Most will prove you wrong, but the ones that don't… you'll be ready for!". We sort of understood this. This is the only time I had ever heard Star swear. I think he was scared.

"Tom," Porlo said. "These portals will take you into any of the most wondrous, marvellous, spectacular dreams you have ever had. But be warned, danger lurks within every single one. Once you are in, you can't get out. Not until you hear the bell chime seven times."

Tom and I slowly got back to our feet. Porlo extended one of his huge golden feathery wings and placed it onto Tom's shoulders. "You do whatever you want to do, Tom," he said.

We looked around at the portals once again. It felt like we were at the point of no return.

Tom looked at Porlo. "I'm ready," he whispered.

"How about you, Sid, are you ready?"

"Yes," I shouted, without hesitation.

"But aren't you coming with us?" Tom asked Porlo.

"I'll be there," he said. "But I doubt you'll recognize me." With that Porlo spread his wings and with two powerful flaps he flew into the air.

"I didn't know you could fly," I shouted to Porlo.

"You never asked," he replied. "See you soon."

With that, Porlo flew out of the cave through one of the portals.

We were alone.

"What do you think, Tom?" I said.

Tom looked at me. He looked ready for anything.

"Let's do it!" he said.

With that we slowly made our way over towards the portal to Lava and Ice.

CHAPTER 8:
INTO THE PORTAL

"You ready?" Tom said as we stood together by the doorway. "I'm ready," I replied.

"On three...Ready... One... Two... Three!"

We held our breath and into the portal we leapt.

Light flashed, loud claps of thunder filled our ears. Tom and I screamed. Before we had time to think we were hurtling down a magma slide from the top of the volcano.

"Hey Tom," a passing camel shouted on the slide next to us. Yes a camel on a magma slide! Soon we were careering off a jump, into an ice tunnel. This was amazing. Three penguins whizzed past us. "Hey guys," they said, "this is awesome, right?"

It was awesome; this was the most fun anyone could ever have. Tom and I were having the time of our lives.

Round and around we went. "This is cranbabulous!" Tom shouted.

Suddenly we looked down and saw the end of the ride. Penguin after polar bear after penguin went crashing into each other as the slide ended over an icy pond that stretched for miles. Thump, thump, thump they went! Cries of joy filled the air as all the wonderful creatures slid out onto the ice.

Soon it was our turn. 'Splat!' We were down. I looked up from my landing position and noticed I had landed on a mass of white fur. "Hey mister," said an amused polar bear in a deep growly voice. "How great was that?"

The polar bear was right. This was great fun! I looked around and Tom was lying next to me with two rockhopper penguins dancing with pure excitement around his head.

"You OK, Tom?" I said.

"OK?" Tom replied, his voice full of excitement. "This was the most amazing thing ever!"

"I agree," I said. "Shall we go again?"

"What do you think!" said Tom, as we skidded and raced our way off the ice towards the top of the volcano.

As we made our way back up, we passed many weird and wonderful creatures.

Snow leopards, reindeer, hundreds and hundreds of penguins, there were even sea lions flapping their way up the pathway to the top.

Suddenly a large red moose with huge horns galloped

past us. "Look at the size of his nostrils!" I said to Tom, laughing. The moose gave us a look. The type of look Mrs Craddlethorpe would give you if you were talking in class. The moose then snorted through its wonderful huge nostrils and carried on running.

I love the word Moose. We had an Uncle in Scotland who called a 'mouse' a 'moose'. He also called a 'house' a 'hoose'. His name is Uncle Christmas. I'm not actually sure whether Uncle Christmas is his real name, but we have always called him this because we only visit him at Christmas time.

We haven't seen him for a long time. It's because Tom finds it hard to see people who remind him of Moon and Star. I feel for Tom sometimes.

Before we knew it we were back at the top of the volcano. "Which slide shall we choose?" Tom yelled, clearly having the most fun ever.

"This one looks good," I shouted back. "It's called the 'Supersonic killer mega savage black hole of doom!'"

This was no ordinary slide. As you looked down from the top, it appeared that you were looking over the edge of a steep cliff.

Up stepped a polar bear. As he stood at the top of the slide he looked rather nervous.

"Are you OK?" Tom asked the now quivering polar bear.

"I feel like crying," he said, his bottom lip trembling.

"Do you know what I do when I'm scared?" said Tom. "I look to my friend Sid, and I talk to him. He always makes me feel better about things."

The polar bear looked unimpressed. "So what does Sid think?" he said.

"I think you should just do it," I said. With that I gently nudged the polar bear and off he went down the slide."

"Cheers, Misteeeeer," the polar bear screamed as he plummeted downwards.

"Do you think he'll be OK, Sid?" Tom asked.

"Of course he will," I replied. "Sometimes people just need a little push in the right direction!"

Tom looked at me with clear excitement in his eyes. "Come on then, let's do it," he said.

With that we leapt onto the magma slide.

"Aaaarrggghhhhhh," we screamed, our arms and legs flapping around as the slide threw us violently from side to side.

"Again!" I shouted, as we crashed into hundreds of furry creatures at the end of the ride.

We leapt up and ran back to the top of the mountain. Down we came. Up we went. Down we came again.

After what seemed like hours and hours of fun we decided to take a break. "I feel a bit sick with all this spinning around," Tom said.

We have been sick a few times in the past. Bizarrely

our old dog Larry always seemed to be sick at the same time as us, although he would often lick Tom's face so this is maybe why. Tom found it strange that when he was sick into the toilet he would get upset and have to lie in bed and drink sips of water and wear a cold flannel on his head (Moon insisted).

But when Larry was sick he would wag his tail and be seemingly the happiest dog in the world. I think people should learn from dogs. Dogs are great, they are simple creatures. People not so much, too complicated.

We looked around for somewhere to sit down and rest. "How about over there?" Tom said.

It appeared to be a café made of ice with many tiny snowmen waiters scurrying around serving drinks.

"Looks good," I replied.

CHAPTER 9:
THE ICE CAFÉ

T he ice café was a hubbub of laughter and chatting, animals were sitting around tables, drinking cooling drinks that had been brought to them by snowmen on roller skates.

"Isn't it wonderful to see all these different animals sitting together having fun?" Tom said.

It was a wonderful sight. Moon and Star would often have their friends over to our old house. We would call them 'Adult Play Dates' or 'APDs'. Tom and I would creep across the landing to the top of the stairs when we were supposed to be sleeping. We would sit there for hours listening to them having fun, telling stories, laughing out loud. It filled us with joy.

We sat down on a table carved out of fresh ice. A tiny snowman with a big carrot nose sped over to us. "Drrrinks?" he asked merrily.

"I'll have a coke please," I said. Tom asked for iced water.

Tom was quiet. He looked thoughtful.

"You OK, Tom?" I asked.

Tom paused. He was still trying to get his head around this magical new world we were in.

"Doesn't this seem weird to you, Sid? All this going on around us, all these talking animals, the volcano, Porlo, the ice, the lava. It seems weird to me," he said.

"It is weird, but magical and fun all squished together," I replied. "Enjoy this time, Tom, you deserve it."

"What do you mean? Why?"

41

I smiled. "Tom. You mean the world to me. You always have, always will. You are kind. You have so much to give. Look at how you dealt with Porlo. I was ready to run out of that cave but you saw the good in him. It is this kindness that makes you special."

Tom smiled. "Sid," he said. "I'm afraid."

"Afraid of what?" I replied.

"I'm afraid of being alone."

"But you'll never be alone. I will always be here with you."

Tom looked down. He was deep in thought.

"I'm close to you, Sid because you're the only person I know I can never lose." His voice seemed full of sadness. "I don't get close to other people because I'm scared they will leave me."

I really felt for Tom, he seemed terribly sad. He seldom spoke about Moon and Star but I know how much he missed them. I placed my hand onto Tom and smiled.

At that moment our drinks arrived. "Thank you very much," Tom said to the tiny snowman. Moon had always told us to be mindful of our manners. "Pllllleasure," the little snowman replied with a huge grin and a tip of the hat. With that he zoomed off to the next ice table.

Tom and I sat together, sipping our drinks. Tom was looking up into the sky. I knew that sometimes the best thing for Tom was to just be close to him. We didn't always need to speak. Sometimes being together was enough.

Suddenly out of nowhere a large bird flew over us. "What is that?" Tom said as he pointed upwards.

Everyone began looking up to the sky. The large bird began circling above the café, darting in and out of the hot molten rocks. "Is that Porlo?" Tom said. "He seems to be losing height!"

"It's coming down," we heard from the table next to us. Panic hit the ice café. The tiny ice snowmen were darting around the tables, collecting ice glasses. The animals were running around in a panic, fleeing the area below.

The bird flapped its wings a few more times, made a fairly exhausted sounding squawking noise, and then fell very ungracefully to the ground.

'Thump' it went as it landed heavily on the ice.

"Curse this stupid ice pond. Why did you pick this portal!" said the bird.

It was golden. It was beautiful. It seemed irritated. It was Porlo!

"PORLO!" we shouted as we ran over, wrapping our arms around his feathery body.

"Are you OK?" asked Tom.

"Nice landing!" I said with a cheeky smile. Porlo looked annoyed. "The landing was faultless!" he said with dignity. "I didn't flatten anyone, did I?" he asked the

43

gathering crowd.

As Porlo slowly got to his feet a small rockhopper penguin lay motionless in a large crater beneath him.

"Oh my days, get this man some water!" Porlo shouted.

As quick as a flash several tiny snowmen appeared with iced water. The penguin raised its head. He looked dazed. "You OK, Giles?" asked Porlo.

"Giles!" I said. "What a ridiculous name for a penguin!"

The penguin looked at Porlo, squinted his eyes, and opened his mouth to speak. "Nice landing," he muttered.

"How many feathers am I holding up?" Porlo asked. Porlo spread out his wing and presented the penguin with hundreds of golden feathers.

"How's he going to count all those?" I asked, rather sarcastically.

"He'll be fine," snapped Porlo. "He's good with maths."

The penguin looked at the feathers. Then looked at Porlo.

"One," he replied, struggling to speak. With that the penguin fell back onto the ice, still visibly dazed and shocked.

"Keep yourself upright, lad," Porlo said, as he lifted the penguin back to his feet.

"Are you sure he's OK?" Tom asked.

"He'll be fine," Porlo replied with a smile, as he turned around and looked at Tom. "How are you, Tom?"

Tom smiled. No words were necessary to describe how we were feeling. Porlo stretched out one of his wonderful golden wings and hugged us both tightly into his large fluffy chest.

"Porlo," I said. "You said that we wouldn't recognise you inside this portal!"

"I tried dressing up as Batman," Porlo replied, sounding slightly irritated, "but you try getting a cape around your neck with no fingers!" With that he sat himself down on one of the ice chairs.

"Seeing you happy is all I wanted," said Porlo, looking around the ice cafe.

Porlo raised his wing into the air and started flapping it around. "Can I get a fizzy ice lemon soda over here?" he shouted.

As quick as a flash a little snowman arrived with Porlo's drink. "One fizzzzy ice lemon soda," he said.

"Oh my days, where is the straw?" Porlo demanded. The snowman lifted off his tiny snowman hat and pulled out a straw from what appeared to be a little storage pot underneath.

"One straw," the little snowman said, with a cheeky grin on his face. The snowman popped the straw into Porlo's glass. "Anyyything else?" the snowman asked cheerfully.

"Just one thing," said Porlo. "Why do you have a carrot as a nose?"

The snowman smiled as he put his hand up to his face, plucked out the carrot, plopped it into Porlo's glass and began stirring his drink. "Voila!" said the little snowman. He seemed pleased with himself.

Porlo smiled. "Brilliant," he said, clearly impressed. The snowman and Porlo began laughing together.

The snowman popped his nose back into his face and skated off to the next table. "Driiiiinks?" we heard in the distance.

CHAPTER 10:
CRABZOIDS

T om, Porlo and I continued chatting in the Ice Café. It felt like Porlo really understood both Tom and me. "Do you have any children?" Tom asked Porlo. "About forty two," Porlo replied. "But they're not called children, they're called eaglets."

I was shocked. "Forty two!"

"I know the names of every single one." Porlo seemed pleased.

"Go on then," I said. "Name them."

Porlo looked deep in thought. "OK. Let me think."

"Bruce, Magnus, Xerxes, Jemima, Theodore, Uma, Mark, Lamar..."

Suddenly the ground began to tremble under our feet. "Can you feel that?" Tom asked. We looked down at the ice. "I can," I said. "It feels like an earthquake."

We looked at Porlo who was still calling out his

47

children's names. He stopped. "It's probably nothing," he replied. "Can I continue now?" He seemed irritated with the interruption.

The ice was beginning to shake more vigorously. Tiny cracks began appearing beneath us.

"Are you sure it's nothing, Porlo?" Tom asked.

Just then we heard a large popping sound directly behind us. As we looked around, we saw a large rock had been catapulted into the air from beneath the ice. The rock rose high into the sky, amongst the hot molten rocks from the volcano.

"Wow, look at that go!" Tom shouted.

As the ice rock rocketed higher into the sky, it collided with one of the hot molten rocks. There was a colossal bang as the ice was instantaneously melted by the heat of the magma rock. From within the ice, a smaller darker rock emerged. This rock fell to the ground, followed by light rain drops created by the ice explosion.

We ran over to where it had landed. "Be careful, Sid," Tom said as I crouched down to take a closer look.

Steam was emanating from the little rock. The heat from the steam was creating a little crater in the ice.

"What do you think it is?" Tom said.

Porlo looked down at the rock. "Stand back," he said, "I think it's hatching!"

Suddenly eight thin, spindly crab-like legs popped

out from underneath the rock. The legs were bent and appeared to have little hairs on them. Two huge claws with large pincers at the ends busted through the front of the rock, followed by two little eyes at the top.

The little eyes moved upwards from the rock, extending out towards Tom, Porlo and me.

The eyes appeared to be following our every movement. I moved my hand up and down in front of the crab-like thing; its eyes followed. "This thing is awesome!" I screamed.

The crab retracted its eyes back into the rock.

"Don't get in its way, Sid," said a concerned Porlo. "Stand in front or behind it and you'll be OK."

"What are they, Porlo?" Tom asked.

"Crabzoids," Porlo replied. "We need to get shelter."

Porlo tucked me under his wing and marched me off towards the shelter of the main café area.

"Driiiinks?" asked one of the little snowmen.

"Not now!" snapped Porlo.

"Quick as you can, Sid," Porlo shouted over to me.

"I'll just be a minute," I replied, still mesmerized by this amazing crab-like creature.

All around us we could hear popping sounds, as the ice rocks continued catapulting their way into the air, followed by loud explosions above us in the sky as the ice was shattered by the magma rocks. More and more rocks were settling into the ice. Each one began hatching into a Crabzoid.

"So what exactly is a Crabzoid" Tom asked.

"Crabzoids are harmless on their own," Porlo said.

"But collectively they are very powerful."

"They seem agitated!" I said, looking at the many Crabzoids that had begun hatching around us.

"You just wait," said Porlo.

Suddenly one of the Crabziods jumped up from the ice and sped past us sideways towards the volcano.

"Wow, they really move!"

Then another Crabzoid did the same. Followed by another. Then another. Then another.

Hundreds of little crabs, running as fast as their little legs would carry them, sideways up the mountain.

"Where are they going?" I asked Porlo.

"Keep looking," he said.

As we looked around the portal we could see it was beginning to change. The sky was becoming dark and stormy. The slides were beginning to disappear. The volcano was being cooled. The ice was melting.

"The elements are causing a neutralising effect," Porlo shouted.

"I've no idea what that means," Tom said.

"It means the ice is heating up, the volcano is cooling."

As the crabs continued to make their way up the mountain, they started to form together, in a large clump. A larger crab shape was beginning to develop at the very top of the volcano.

"Is this what you meant Porlo?" Tom said. "Is this how they create their power?"

"Yes, Tom." Porlo seemed very concerned.

By now all the animals in the portal had gathered within the shelter of the ice café.

There was one exception: me!

"Sid, come over here to safety! What are you doing?" Tom shouted.

"I can't get back, Tom!" I replied. Every time I tried to move another Crabzoid would scamper past me, blocking my path to the ice café. "What happens if I tread on one, Porlo?"

"If you're lucky it'll go crunch! But I wouldn't risk it," replied Porlo. "If you get it wrong you'll be whisked off towards the mountain. Once they've got you you'll struggle to get away."

"So what should I do?"

Tom looked around. He seemed determined. "Don't worry, Sid, I'm coming."

Without hesitation he ran towards me.

Suddenly "STOP!" boomed a large voice right next to Tom, as a large white furry arm reached over and pulled him back. "It's too dangerous!"

Tom looked up. He instantly recognised him. It was a polar bear. It was the same polar bear that Tom had tried to help at the top of the magma slide. The polar bear looked down his wonderfully long white nose at Tom. "I'll help with this," he said, in a deep growly voice.

"You're not big enough!"

With that the polar bear turned around and began walking across the melting ice towards me. The polar bear was big, really big. He had huge feet. Every time he trod on the ground there was a large crunching sound as a Crabzoid was crushed beneath him.

Porlo leant over and whispered in my ear, "I'll eat those crab remains later," he said, licking his lips.

"This is no time for tummy talk, Porlo. My best friend is in danger!" Tom said. He seemed annoyed.

The polar bear had now reached me. "Put out your hand, friend," he said.

I stretched my hand towards the polar bear, but as I did so I lost my balance on the ice and fell to the floor. I tried to get back to my feet but it was too late. The Crabzoids had me in their grasp.

"Help me, Tom!" I shouted.

Before I knew it I was being carried up the mountain path towards the volcano.

CHAPTER 11:
THE ALPHA CRAB

T om looked around to Porlo. "What should I do?"

"Follow your instincts, Tom."

Tom paused. He looked down at the scampering crustaceans, and then looked back at Porlo.

"Ok," he said. "Here goes."

With that, Tom jumped onto a bunch of passing Crabzoids. He was heading for the mountain too. "I'm coming, Sid," he shouted.

"Tom. They are taking you to the Alpha Crab," Porlo shouted. "Confuse it if you can, but mind the giant claws." By now his voice had become distant.

It almost felt like we were surfing up the mountain, the little Crabzoids acting like surf boards beneath us. I put my arms out to help keep my balance. Tom was just behind me doing the same. "Keep calm, Sid," he shouted to me.

By now I was within touching distance of the Alpha Crab. The scurrying Crabzoids beneath my feet darted away, dropping me to the floor with a thud. I looked up. It was right there in front of me. Its huge claws were suspended motionless above my head. I stood up; as I did so the two huge eyes on the Alpha Crab extended out from its head and peered down at me on the floor.

I could hear a faint rumbling sound. It was the noise of its colossal claws moving right above my head. The gigantic pincers at the end of one of its huge claws opened up, moved down over me and clamped shut. I was trapped. "Help!" I screamed.

Just then Tom arrived; he jumped off the Crabzoids and stood in front of the Alpha.

The crab lowered its other claw downwards, trying to swipe at Tom. Tom jumped as high as he could straight onto the crab's giant pincer. As fast as he could, he ran up its claw onto its head, just behind its two huge eyes. Tom stood up. The crab seemed confused. It tried to extend its eyes towards the back of its head but to no avail.

Tom was out of sight of the Alpha crab.

"What are you doing, Tom?" I shouted.

"Trust me, Sid," he replied. "Just try not to get eaten!"

"Try not to get eaten!" I screamed in response. "That's reassuring! Trust me, I don't want to be crab food!"

The Alpha Crab had become really agitated, claws

flailing as it tried to get Tom off its head.

It began to extend out its eight large legs and slowly stood up.

Tom began running around on top of the crab. The crab seemed confused. It began lifting its claws, in an effort to knock Tom off its head, throwing me around as it did so.

"Next time he raises his claws grab onto me," Tom shouted.

"But he's gripping me too hard," I replied.

"Just reach out as far as you can," Tom said, as he continued jumping and running around on top of the crab. The crab threw its claws higher and higher, trying to knock Tom off its head; each time I would extend my hand out towards him, but to no avail.

"This time, Sid," Tom shouted. "Try really hard to reach me." As the crab threw its claw up I reached out to Tom. I stretched as hard as I could towards his waiting hand.

We touched.

In that split second we closed our hands as tightly as we could.

"Don't let go," Tom screamed.

But the crab was not letting go either, and was much stronger than both Tom and me. Tom was dragged off the top of the crab, still holding tightly onto my hands.

The crab began throwing us up and down in an almost juggling type motion.

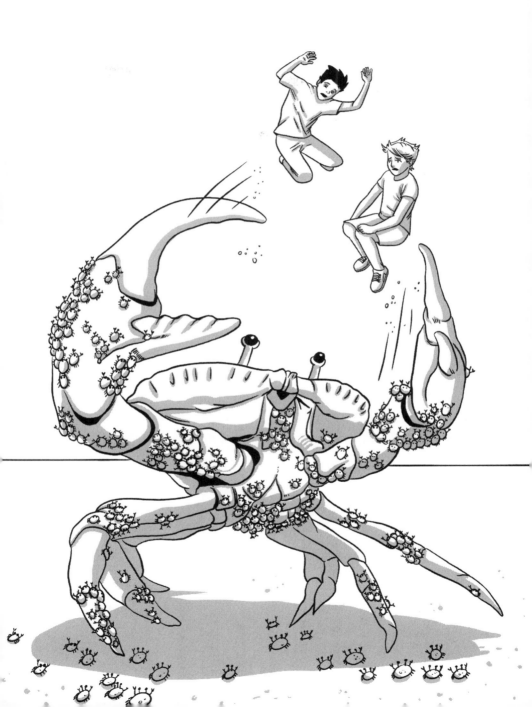

We had failed.

"What's going to happen, Tom?" I shouted.

Our arms and legs were being tossed around in the air like rag dolls. The Alpha Crab seemed to be playing around with us, throwing us up with one claw and catching us with the other.

The crab seemed angry. Its pincers were moving inwards towards its face.

It began to open its mouth.

"It's going to eat us?" I shouted.

Tom was staring upwards towards the sky.

The crab's mouth was now fully open. It tossed us up into the air one more time and moved its claws out of the way so we could fall freely into its huge gaping mouth.

I closed my eyes, and awaited my fate.

Suddenly I felt something take hold of me. I was no longer falling. I opened my eyes and looked down. The Alpha Crab was beneath me. It looked angrier than ever! I looked across. There was Tom. He was next to me, holding onto a large claw! I looked up.

"SQQQQQQWWWWWAAAAARRRRRK!" we heard.

Followed by, "Oh my days, how heavy are you!"

It was Porlo.

"PORLO!" I shouted. I looked at Tom. He was smiling.

"Now that was close!" Tom said. "Was it going to eat us?"

"Who knows?" Porlo replied. "Probably!"

We flew high into the sky, Porlo gripping us tightly with his legs. The portal was changing below us. The magma rocks had disappeared. The ice had melted away.

"What about the Alpha Crab?" Tom asked. "What's going to happen to all the animals down there – they must be in danger?"

Porlo smiled. "Always thinking of others, Tom," he replied. "They'll be fine. The Alpha just needs feeding. Once he's eaten, the Crabzoids will have eaten too and they will disperse."

"What will he eat?" Tom asked.

"Once the ice has melted, the water is full of fish and algae. He'll feast. As will the rest of us."

Porlo placed us down at the top of the mountain. In front of us I could see the portal door.

Porlo smiled. "You just saved your best friend, Tom." Porlo put his golden wing around Tom's shoulder.

"No I didn't," he replied. "You did!"

"Sid would have been eaten way before I arrived if you hadn't've been there, Tom. If you hadn't shown such bravery. You had no hesitation in running after your friend." He seemed almost proud.

We made our way back to the portal exit.

"You didn't know this, Tom, but you can't be harmed in this portal."

"Why not?" I asked.

"This portal has no effect on people from the outside world. It can't harm you. But Sid, he is different. He is part of you. But not the part that the outside world sees."

"So none of this is real, Porlo?"

"It's real to us, Tom," Porlo replied. "But you didn't know that when you risked your life to help your best friend. He was in danger. You didn't think twice about the consequences. You just did it. You were brave."

Tom looked at me. I was quiet. I looked back at him. I smiled. "Thank you, Tom," I said.

I stood up and walked over towards Tom. We were face to face. It felt like I was looking at myself in the mirror. We hugged. "Tom. This is hard to say." I felt upset.

"What is it, Sid?" Tom said.

"I'm staying here. I'm staying in the portals, with Porlo. I will always be with you, Tom. But you are ready, ready to live your life."

"But, Sid," Tom said. "I can't be without you!"

"You'll never be without me, Tom. You've never really been without me and you never will. We are one, Tom. I'll always be there. You've proved you are strong. You've not needed me at all since we came into this portal.

"But I know this isn't real, Sid," Tom said. "When have you ever seen penguins on a water slide!"

I heard a clock chime.

Tom looked at me. Nothing else needed to be said.

Porlo gave Tom a huge squeeze. The type of squeeze where your eyes nearly pop out of their sockets.

"Now go, Tom," Porlo said. "Run as fast as you can back home."

The clock chimed a second time, and a third and a fourth.

Tom took one last look around the portal. It had changed so much since we had arrived. We could see the ice café in the distance. It was melting, but all the wonderful animals were standing there waving to us.

"Goodbye," Tom shouted.

With that he jumped through the portal door. The thunder clapped around us as he entered the portal chamber.

Tom ran.

He ran as fast as he could down the cave. Two further clock chimes rang out.

Tom ran out of the cave, under the large rock. He tiptoed his way across the little rocks in the stream. By now his shoes were capped in mud.

He ran through the clearing in the dark forest, knelt down and crawled his way towards the light forest.

As fast as he could he ran towards our house.

Tom opened the front door; he was trying not to make

a sound. Tom slipped off his muddy shoes and tiptoed upstairs. There was no sign of Uncle Jack or Auntie Jayne. They must have been asleep.

As quietly as he could he slid into bed, put on his pyjamas, and lay there.

Tom closed his eyes.

CHAPTER 12:

BECOMING ONE

*T*he seventh chime rang out.

I opened my eyes and looked around.

"Are you here, Sid?" I whispered quietly. I could feel my heart beating in my chest.

There was no reply. I could sense Sid was with me but I was alone.

I could see through my bedroom door onto the landing where Uncle Jack's old grandfather clock was faintly echoing, having just completed its final chime. It was seven o'clock. I looked across to my window. The sun was beginning to rise. It was morning.

Suddenly I heard footsteps from outside my room, followed by a gentle tapping at my bedroom door. "Can we come in?" It was Uncle Jack and Auntie Jayne. "Yes," I replied, as I started to sit up in bed, wiping the sleep from my eyes.

"Happy Birthday, Tom," Uncle Jack said as the two of them entered my room with booming smiles. "Ten today, little man."

Auntie Jayne had a tear in her eye but she looked happy. "We have a special gift for you," Auntie Jayne said as she sat down on the end of my bed and reached into a rather large carrier bag.

"For me?" I said, as Auntie Jayne placed a small wooden box in front of me.

"Yes, Tom." She looked up at Uncle Jack. "It's from your mum and dad."

"Something from Moon and Star!" I was shocked.

I looked at Auntie Jayne's smiling face. I loved her smile. Moon had a similar smile which lit me up every time I saw it. I looked at the present. In some ways I didn't want to open it. I wanted to savour this moment. It was a moment that somehow brought me close to my parents. I closed my eyes. Auntie Jayne put her hand into mine and we held each other. I had goose bumps all over my body.

Sid and I love the words 'Goose Bumps'. We would always imagine lots of geese in blindfolds bumping into each other and laughing and having fun as they fell onto their bums. Sid fills me with joy. I love him.

"Take as long as you like, Tom," Auntie Jayne said. I looked over at Uncle Jack. I think he had put some more weight on around his tummy. I know what Sid would say if he were here. He'd tell Uncle Jack that he looked a little portly. I didn't care. Uncle Jack knew that I loved him. "Your tummy looks a little bigger," I said to Uncle Jack with a smile.

Uncle Jack chuckled. "That'll be your Auntie Jayne's steak and kidney pies," he said. He didn't seem to mind at all as he patted his belly three or four times.

It made me think that maybe I should be like Sid a little more often. I understood what was right and wrong but sometimes it's ok to say cheeky things. I felt happy.

"Would you like to be alone?" Uncle Jack said.

"No," I replied. "I want you here if that's OK."

"Of course it is," Auntie Jayne replied as she leant over and put her hand on my face. She had really soft hands.

I lifted up my present. "It's really heavy," I said, clasping it tightly.

"Be a little careful with it, Tom," Uncle Jack said.

There was a card attached to the present.

I opened it. It read: *'Happy birthday to our beloved son. May all your dreams come true? Love Mum and Dad xxx'*

"Can you give us a minute please?" Auntie Jayne said as she looked up at Uncle Jack.

Uncle Jack smiled and walked out of my bedroom. He pulled the door until it was nearly closed.

"Auntie Jayne?"

"Yes," she replied as she lifted my hand up to her face. "What is it, Tom?"

"Can we go and see Uncle Christmas again soon? I miss him."

"Of course we can, Tom," she replied. She seemed really happy. "Why don't we call him later today and you can chat on the phone. He'd love to see you."

"Do you think I could go and see Uncle Leonard too?"

"I may need a little longer to sort that one, Tom," she replied. "But I'm sure it will be fine." She seemed even happier. She started crying again.

"Why are you crying?" I asked. "It makes me cry when you cry."

"I'm sorry Tom," she replied, "but you remind me so much of your mum sometimes. She would be so proud, especially today on your tenth birthday."

I paused. "What was she like?" I asked.

Auntie Jayne looked like she was sifting through her brain to find the exact answer.

"She was just like you," she said, wiping away her tears. "A little shy but a heart of pure gold, so kind."

"How about my dad?" I asked.

"He was confident." She nodded her head and smiled. I could tell she was thinking about him. "Maybe even a little brash sometimes. But funny. He loved an adventure. But most of all he loved you so much. They both did."

I looked down towards my present and re-read the gift tag.

"I miss them," I said.

"I know," Auntie Jayne replied.

I lay in my bed, holding onto Auntie Jayne's hand.

It was time.

"I'm going to open it," I said. My tummy was turning over and over.

I gently opened the small wooden box and put my hand inside. It felt cold. I slowly lifted it out. "I'm going to love it, whatever it is!" I said.

As I saw the gift I gasped. It was beautiful.

It was the shiniest, most beautiful dazzling golden eagle I had ever seen.

"Porlo!" I whispered to myself. I smiled. I loved it.

"Can I tell you a true story?" Auntie Jayne said. "When you were nearly five your mum and dad took you to the zoo. Do you remember?"

"Yes I do," I replied. "Star would pretend the animals could talk and do all these funny voices. We were all laughing. I loved it."

"Well. Do you remember your favourite animal that day?"

"Yes, it was an eagle. I remember. I loved the eagle. He looked so fierce but when the man touched him he was gentle. He had little babies in his nest which he was caring for."

"That was just before your fifth birthday, Tom. On that day your mum and dad brought you this special gift. We thought it might be a little easier for you to have this now you are ten."

I looked up at Auntie Jayne. "Can I be alone now?"

"Of course you can," she replied. With that Auntie Jayne stood up and made her way over to my bedroom door. She paused.

"Oh, there is one more thing, Tom. Have a look in the middle." She smiled again and pulled the door closed behind her.

I looked down towards the eagle. I clasped it firmly with both hands and pulled as hard as I could. The eagle slowly opened up.

Just then a little red pendant fell out of the middle of the eagle on to the bed covers in front of me.

The pendant was in the shape of a heart. There was some text inscribed on one side. It read 'I am Porlo, Guardian of Memories'. I turned the heart over. On the other side there was a picture. It was taken in the zoo that day. It was a picture of me. I was standing in the middle of Moon and Star. They are hugging me so hard my face is squished in between them.

The memory of the day at the zoo was wonderful. I held the heart close to my chest. I turned onto my side and put my head back onto my pillow.

It was Saturday morning. No school for two whole days. "Yes!" I said to myself, as I pulled a mini fist pump!

I felt tired. I closed my eyes.

"Tom, welcome back," Sid said. "Porlo's got his foot stuck in quicksand in the pyramid of doom portal. We need your help!"

I looked at my best friend and felt happy.

"Happy Birthday, Sid," I said.

"Happy Birthday, Tom," he replied.

My name is Tommy Cockle. My best friend is called Sid. We are inseparable.

THE END

Supporting:

Child Bereavement UK supports families and educates professionals when a
baby or child of any age dies or is dying, or when a child is facing bereavement.

Our vision is for all families to have the support they need to
rebuild their lives, when a child grieves or when a child dies.

We aim to ensure the accessibility of high quality child bereavement
support and information to all families and professionals
by increasing our reach and plugging the gaps that exist in
bereavement support and training across the country.

www.childbereavementuk.org

Helpline: *0800 02 888 40*